States, in Order to form a more perfect Union, establish Justice,

general Welfare, and secure the Blessings of Liberty to ourselves

States of America.

gress of the United States, which shall consist of a Senate and House

oren every second Year by the People of the several States, and the Electors

ranch of the State Legislature.

ge of twenty-five Years, and been seven Years a Citizen of the United States,

chosen.

tes which may be included within this Union, according to their respective

including those bound to Service for a Term of Years, and excluding Indians

within three Years after the first Meeting of the Congress of the United States,

aw direct. The Number of Representatives shall not exceed one for every

such enumeration shall be made, the State of New Hampshire shall be

titled to one; Connecticut five, New York six, New Jersey four, Pennsylvania

Published in Burbank, California, by Warner Bros. Worldwide Publishing.
4000 Warner Boulevard, Burbank, California 91522.

Book designed by David Kaestle, Inc.
Packaged by David Kaestle, Inc., New York, New York.
Art direction by Allen Helbig.
Edited by Charles Carney.
Production and printing managed by Gina Misiroglu.
Film separations by Final Film, Los Angeles, California.


Library of Congress Cataloging-in-Publication Data

Jones, Chuck, 1912-
     Daffy Duck for president / written and illustrated by Chuck Jones.
          p.     cm.
     Summary: While lobbying for a year-long open season on rabbits,
Daffy Duck discovers how the constitutional system of checks and
balances protects democracy in the United States.
     ISBN 1-890371-00-9 (alk.paper)
     [1. United States—Politics and government—Fiction.
2. Separation of powers—Fiction. 3. Ducks—Fiction. 4. Rabbits–
–Fiction.]    I. Title.
PZ7.J6825Daf   1997
[E]—dc21                                                      97–9528
                                                                CIP
                                                                 AC


ISBN  1-890371-00-9
Printed in the United States of America.
1 2 3 4 5 6 7 8 9—99 98 97 96

# Written and Illustrated by
## Chuck Jones™

I'm in the money, I'll skin the bunny...

I'll squash the rabbit...make it a habit...

I've got a lot of what it takes to change the law! Ta-tya-ta-da-da . . .

Old man rabbit, you done me wrong...I've got a lot of what it takes
to get along...ya-ha-ha-huh-uh-huh...

Dum-de-de-dum-dum-ya-ha-ha-dee-dee-da-dee-dah . . .

Eh, what's up – *duck*?

*What's up*, is it? I'll tell you what's up—when I'm President, I'm gonna pass a law that'll outlaw rabbits!

*That*, my poor unfortunate soon-to-be-condemned species is "what is up"!

Very ingenious solution to a long-smoldering problem, but there's just one slight tech-a-nicality...

The President can't pass laws.

The President can't pass WHAT?
That's ridiculous!

The President can do anything, *anything* he wants! He's just like a king, only…only…*better!*

Eh, he's better, all right — but he's no king.

Says so right here, good buddy. You're outnumbered by the Founding Fathers. It's the number one law of the United States, of which we is lawful citizens.

Give me that! Who wrote this? Foundling Fathers, indeed!
Bunch of mewling infants, no doubt!

Right. "Infants" like George Washington, James Madison, Ben Franklin, Alexander Hamilton. Read on, McDuck . . .

Hmmmm . . . let's just see here . . . Hmmmm . . . oh, yeah? Ben Washington. Well, hmmmmm . . . Whattya know—heh! *Congress* makes the laws. The President has to sign 'em and enforce 'em.

Pardon me whilst I pause for a moment of reflection.

Washington . . . Congress makes the laws . . . year-round
rabbit season . . . Congress, hmmm, Congress . . . *that's* the ticket!

Good luck, pal. There've been a lot of innocent people sent to Congress, but you may be the first *lame duck* to be *elected*.

Watch yer manners, buster! You are addressing the
Right Honorable Congressman Duck—soon-to-be, that is.

No more duck seasons! From now on, only *rabbits* are sitting ducks!

# DAILY BLAT

# UNKNOWN MALLARD ELECTED TO CONGRESS!

*Elected Rep. D. Delano Duck*
*States 3,000,000 Long Island Ducklings*
*Can't Be Wrong!!!*

*HAH!*

Congressmen! Senators! All those in favor of
universal suffrage—instead of suffering—for all ducks, and
a 365-day hunting season for rabbits, say "AYE!"

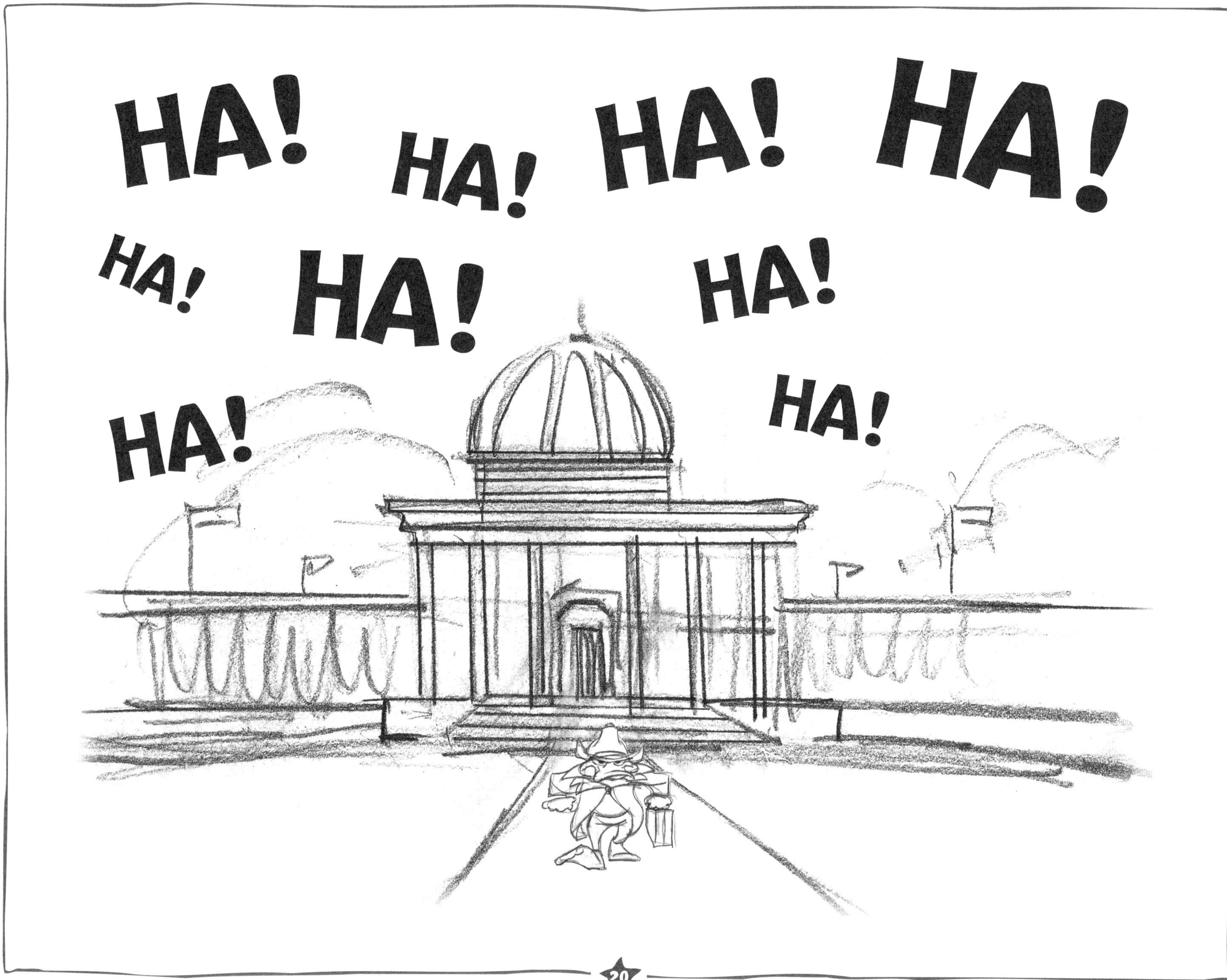
HA!
HA!
HA!
HA!
HA!
HA!
HA!
HA!
HA!

Can you imagine anything so ridiculous as majority rule?

Loop-hole, loop-hole, my kingdom for a loop-hole ... mmm ... Congress makes the laws, the President puts them to work, and ...

Yaaawn!

... and ... and ... and the *courts* interpret them ...

That's it! What we need around here is a little interpretation!

And who better to interpret a law about *rabbits* than a *duck*?!

Okay, cottontail. I'm taking the whole duck season/rabbit season stuff...

...to the Supreme Court to abja...apra...to abrag...to decide in my favor!

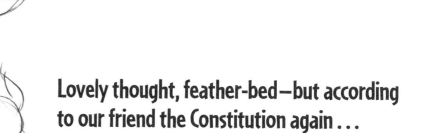

Lovely thought, feather-bed—but according to our friend the Constitution again...

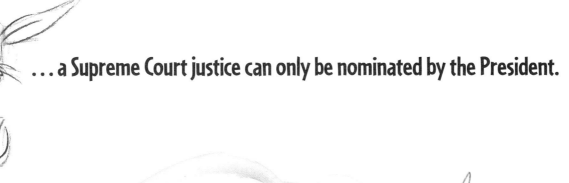

... a Supreme Court justice can only be nominated by the President.

SLAP!
SLAP!

Let's see. The President can't make laws, so that's out. Congress can make laws, but they won't interpret them, so that's out. The Supreme Court interprets laws, but I can't swing that unless the President nominates me ...

What I wanna know is ...

**WHO'S RUNNING THIS COUNTRY, ANYWAY?**

*We* are. We citizens vote, and our leaders work to uphold the laws or at the next election we vote again and get new leaders who will. Look at the bright side, pal. You've learned a lot about why one mallard with a mission can't take over the American system. It's rigged to protect itself.

And, eh, now you've got an idea of how to get along in a democracy. Seize the day, duck.

Well, if at first you don't succeed, seize, seize again.

# We the People

of the Un...

insure domestic Tranquility, provide for the common defence, prom...
and our Posterity, Do ordain and establish this Constitution for the...

## Article. I.

Section. 1. All legislative Powers herein granted shall be vested in...
of Representatives.

Section. 2. The House of Representatives shall be composed of Mem...
in each State shall have the Qualifications requisite for Electors of the most numer...

No Person shall be a Representative who shall not have attained t...
and who shall not, when elected, be an Inhabitant of that State in which he s...

Representatives and direct Taxes shall be apportioned among the seven...
Numbers, which shall be determined by adding to the whole Number of free...
not taxed, three fifths of all other Persons. The actual Enumeration shall...
and within every subsequent Term of ten Years, in such Manner as they sha...
thirty Thousand, but each State shall have at Least one Representative; an...
entitled to chuse three; Massachusetts eight; Rhode Island and Providenc...